KIBBLE KREW AND THE CASTLE ON NORTH HILL

VIBHA CHETHAN

ISBN 979-888569158-1

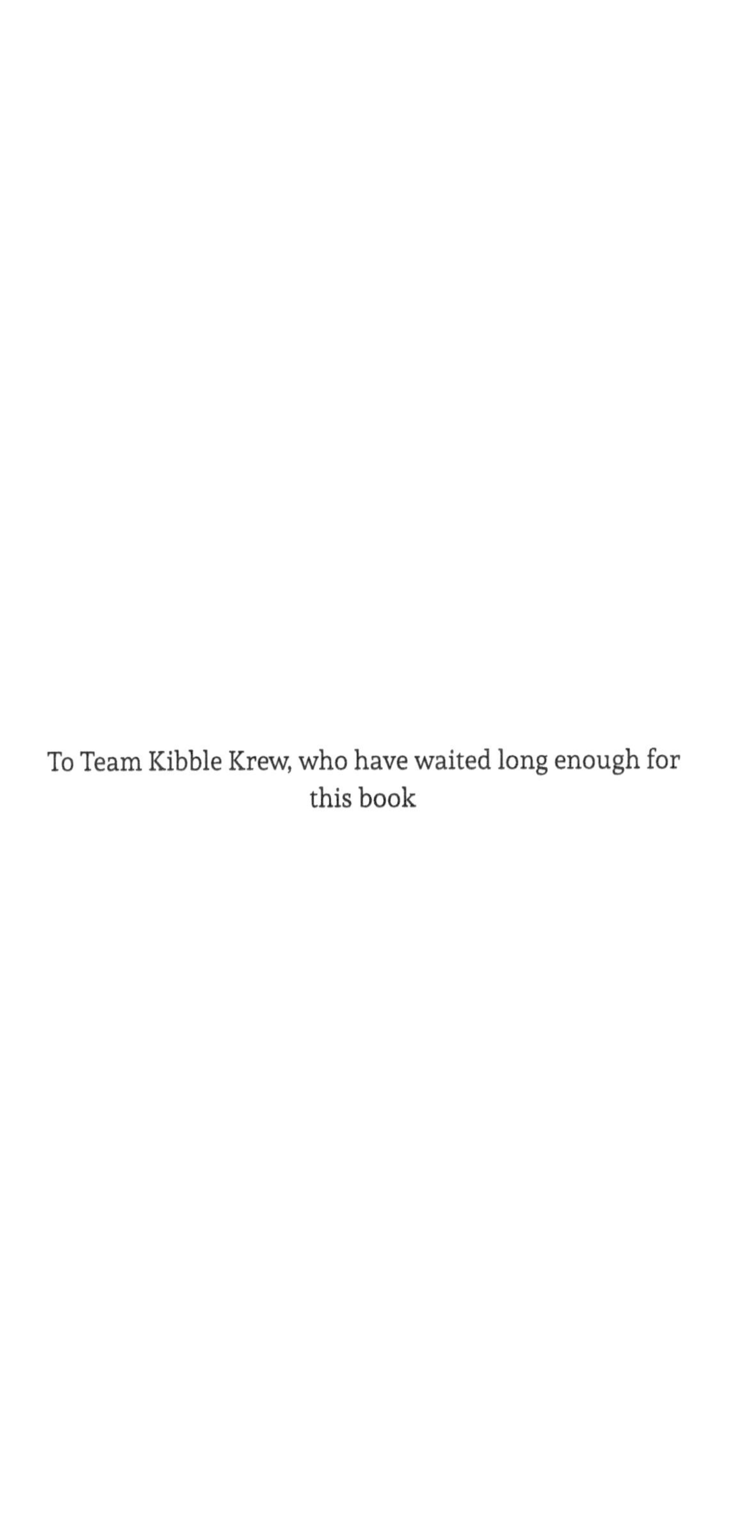

To Team Kibble Krew, who have waited long enough for this book

Contents

Preface

Team Kibble Krew came together because of the four dogs. We became friends immediately and our friendship is what inspired me to write a book dedicated to this group. We all have cherished moments together and this book will be a reminder to all of those memories we made together.

Acknowledgements

I'd like to thank my parents and sister Paris for always supporting me and motivating me while I wrote this story. I'd also like thank my dear friend Captain Jennifer, who helped me take inspiration from small things around and of course the dogs and the rest of my friends for being the reason I wrote this story. I'd also like thank my uncle who helped me with the editing and vocabulary. I would like to pay tribute to Late Pacho through this story, he was a dog we found on the streets but unfortunately his time with us was limited and he inspired the character of Lian in this story. You will be remebered dear friend.

ONE

It's summer break for Team Kibble Krew and they are on PuppyCove Island enjoying the lush greenery and the sound of waves on the shore. The members of this group, ask? Captain Jennifer. The leader of this group, she's got a dog named Mr.WigglyButt. Her two children, Harry and Sasha are also a part of the group. They both love playing basketball just like their teammate Scarlett. She too has a dog named Mr.Marshmallow and he is very jumpy and excited to meet new people. Jade and Caroline are up next. Both of them don't have dogs so they decided to stick with Team Kibble Krew. In-fact both of them happen to be scared of dogs and try to stay away as much as possible but the dogs are just so adorable that they can't stop themselves from playing with them. Alex and Paris are our second sibling pair. Alex loves playing instruments while Paris loves dancing. Both of them have different personalities. Alex is a free bird and loves writing and reading books while Paris is a responsible one with little to no interest in books or writing. Though their interests might differ they love dogs all the same. Katie and Ashley being our third sibling pair have a dog named Mr.Chocos. Mr.Chocos loves to make Ashley run as he chases squirrels on PuppyCove Island and Katie the cool bird, just sits around laughing at her elder sister. Again this sibling pair has different interests and personalities. Ashley is the worrywart while Katie is a jumpy and fun loving girl who enjoys her time. Sage cannot be forgotten! After all her dog Mr.Miles is the eldest of this group! Sage loves adventure, she and Mr.Miles have a lot of fun running free on the grounds just outside Kibble Krew's cottage. Mr.Miles' tiny legs slow him down but he enjoys himself anyway. As a group Team Kibble Krew is always up for some fun!

TWO

Since Team Kibble Krew is always up for some fun they decided to go camping by the lake near North Hill. They had just finished school and were on summer vacation. They wanted to go camping and spend time with Captain Jennifer and their dogs who they had missed a lot because they were busy with classes. So, they woke up early on Saturday and packed up their bags. They had breakfast and immediately left for the woods. The children rode the horses and Captain Jennifer gave a ride to the dogs in her black jeep. It was afternoon when they reached the lake near North Hill. Everyone soon got very busy setting up their tents and helping others to do the same. Captain Jennifer then took out a few utensils to cook some food. They gathered around to find out what was for lunch. They were making some grilled chicken tacos!! The elder kids, Ashley, Alex and Harry helped Captain Jennifer with the cooking while the younger ones ran out playing near the lake. The dogs were basking in the sun enjoying the cool breeze. After a while all the tacos were cooked and served. The kids devoured them immediately. The dogs had fresh fruits for lunch. Later after lunch they decided to play some games. They played tag, hide and seek and just talked about missing the island. So it was evening and they really wanted to take a dip in the lake so they jumped in and splashed water on each other and had a blissful time together. Soon it got dark and Captain Jennifer called them to change and help her with the food. Alex and Ashely changed fast and ran to help Captain Jennifer. They made tofu salad and Miso soup. They all loved it. After they had dinner, they sat around the bonfire. Alex took out his little ukulele and Captain Jennifer handed out skewers and marshmallows. They stuck their marshmallows and put them over the fire while Alex played some songs. After some songs Scarlett suggested that they should play 'Mafia' But Alex didn't understand the game and he just wanted to take a walk around. Captain Jennifer agreed and told not to go far. They started playing the game and having fun but Alex on the other hand was absorbed in looking at the moon in the dark sky and ended up walking too far away. That's when he noticed an old castle-like figure on the North Hill.

THREE

Seeing the old ruined figure in the light he thought he should tell the others so he ran back to the campsite. He reached the campsite panting. The other kids were laughing and enjoying the stories. They all looked at Alex and asked him to sit with them but Alex walked up to Captain Jennifer and whispered something in her ear. Immediately the other kids saw her eyes widen after hearing what Alex said. She stood up and said "Guys! Guess what? Alex has found us some adventure!! He saw a castle on North Hill! We could go and see it tomorrow!!". The kids looked at Alex. He nodded back and they shouted together "Yes!". Alex joined the others and continued listening to the stories told by Captain Jennifer. After a while Captain Jennifer finished her last story. The kids wanted to hear more but Captain Jennifer ran out of stories. They started to wonder what to do when Mr.WigglyButt jumped at Captain Jennifer and they had new entertainment. The dogs wanted to play ball and hide and seek. They started playing hide and seek. The dogs were quick to find their owners but took a while to find the others. After playing hide and seek for a while they sat and rested for a few minutes and went back to play ball. After they had finished playing everything they washed themselves clean and sat around the bonfire to get warmed up before hitting the sack. They sat and talked for a while about how classes had been and then went to their respective tents with the dogs and fell asleep. Captain Jennifer was just looking up at the dark night sky admiring the beauty of nature. She felt happy that the kids were back and they could enjoy their summer vacations together as a group. She smiled at herself and winded up a few things and packed them up for tomorrow. After cleaning up she went to check the kids. She found Alex reading a book in the tent while Paris was asleep. She checked on the other and told Alex to sleep. She herself went to her tent to get a good night's sleep for they had to explore the castle the next day.

FOUR

The next day Captain Jennifer was the first to wake up. She got up with her dog, Mr.WigglyButt and went to the lake to freshen up. The lake's water was very cold and Mr.WigglyButt enjoyed drinking it. Captain Jennifer came back and sat near the almost-dead bonfire and lit it up to warm her morning coffee. The kids were woken up by whistling of the kettle. They ran out of their tents excited to explore the castle and ignoring the cold water they freshened up quickly and helped Captain Jennifer to make breakfast. They had campfire cinnamon rolls and campfire sandwiches. They were lip smacking. After their little breakfast they clean the pans and pots they used and packed everything up. They loaded everything into the jeep and the dogs climbed in. Captain Jennifer was ready and the kids mounted their horses and rode off towards the North Hill. They found a grand decorated staircase that had worn out a bit over the years. They got down from their horses and Captain Jennifer got out of the jeep with the dogs and handed them over to the owners. Then leaving their horses and jeep below they walked up the grand staircase. The dogs were excited about being in the new place, even the kids were surprised. There was an enormous lawn area and it was covered in dry and dead shrubs and bushes. There were a few trees that were actually surviving but ignoring them the group walked in to find a large door. They opened it up and Paris' worst nightmare had come true. There were cobwebs literally everywhere. She hated spiders.She hated cobwebs. They walked into the magnificent castle to find another grand but dusty staircase leading up to a hundred different rooms. Besides the rooms they found a kitchen and dining room to the left side of the grand staircase and a ballroom towards the right side. They walked up the staircase and walked into a room which seemed like the living room. The dogs had already jumped onto the dusty chairs fighting for the best one. The group laughed at how adorable the dogs were. They wanted to explore the rest of the castle and decided to go to the other rooms But Paris said that she'd stay with the dogs in the living room as she was already tired of the cobwebs. The rest of the group left the room and Paris dusted a chair and sat.

FIVE

As Paris waited in the living room with the dogs, the rest of the group moved forward to find a museum-like place and walked around the dusty place seeing portraits of a young man and his wife with their dogs. Captain Jennifer felt as though she had seen those two faces somewhere before but she couldn't remember where. She tried hard to recall but couldn't. Tired, she and the group walked into the next room where there were different artefacts kept in tall glass showcases. There were Chinese dolls, marble statues and photo frames of the same couple with a child and dog. The picture confused Captain Jennifer as she tried to recall where she had seen the couple and when she had seen them but she failed to recall. They moved on to the next room. It was filled with books so it was a library. The kids walked around grabbing random books to read and sat down at the tables to read them. Sasha picked up a fairytale book and read the author's name "Dorothy Sabestian" she said and to Captain Jennifer's surprise it was her mother's name! Even Sasha and Harry knew that it was their grandmother's name. Captain Jennifer asked Sasha to read a few stories and immediately she realised that the stories were told to her by her mother when she was younger. She went back to the room where she saw the photo frame and took out a photo of her mother and father on her phone and compared both of them. She knew immediately that the couple were actually her parents and the kid was herself. She walked back into the library and Alex brought a big book in front of her and told her that the castle actually belonged to her parents. Captain Jennifer was pleasantly surprised and decided to video call her mother in Hamstone City. On the video call she showed Grandma Dorothy that she and kids were in the castle and Grandma Dorothy said nothing but "I'm coming" and she ended the call. The kids and Captain Jennifer were puzzled and decided to go to the cottage and wait for Grandma Dorothy. They packed up and took off on their horses and Captain Jennifer wasn't far behind.

SIX

They parked the jeep and left the horses in the stable. They went into the house and rested while waiting for Grandma. Soon they heard the bell and opened the door to Grandma Dorothy standing in the doorway. Captain Jennifer hugged her tight and welcomed her in. She put off her coat and bags to the side and took a seat on the couch. Harry got her some water to drink. She drank up and called all of them to sit around her. Once all of them were sitting comfortably she said "So, I know you guys found the castle. So congratulations! But I knew about the castle all along. I just didn't tell you guys because I wanted you to have a little adventure finding it. Well now that you've found it, let's see what we can do about it. How about we renovate it and we can use it!" The kids and Captain Jennifer agreed to what Grandma said with disbelief. They started discussing things among themselves until Grandma spoke up again. "I do notice that the sun is right above our heads, I wonder who wants some amazing pesto pasta." Everyone looked at each other and said loudly "Yes!!! We want some pesto pasta!!!" Grandma smiled and got up to go to the kitchen. In the kitchen she put on her apron and started grabbing things from the kitchen. She got pine nuts, some olive oil, pasta, some parmesan cheese, salt and pepper. She noticed that the main ingredients were missing!! The fresh basil and garlic needed to be harvested from their little herb garden in the backyard of the cottage. Harry and Caroline went to get the garlic and basil for the pasta. Alex and Paris helped Grandma Dorothy with boiling the pasta, cutting the garlic and basil and of course grating the cheese. Katie, Sasha, Jade and Scarlett were playing with the dogs. Sage on the other hand was very quiet. She was reading a book with Ashley. Captain Jennfier was in the stables feeding hay to the horses. Grandma took her time to make the pasta and served the dish to them. All of them took a bite and their eyes widened. They never had such a delicious and lip smacking pasta ever. After all, Grandma Dorothy owned a restaurant in Hamstone City.

SEVEN

After lunch they tidied up and sat together in the living room. They came up with a plan as to what they could do to the castle. The very first thing on their long to-do list was dusting the entire place. They decided to go to Hamstone City the very next day to buy cleaning agents and detergents. After the first task was getting the electronics fixed so that they have enough lights working for them to stay back in the castle at night. The third task was to give all the sheets and cushions to the dry cleaners to have them cleaned and tidied and the fourth task was to get the couch and chair covering fixed since they were torn and destroyed by mites and fleas. Fifth task on the list was to clean the curtains. They thought about any more tasks they had to get done and Harry pointed out that the garden needed to be cleared out so that they could plant new plants. So the seventh task was to clear out dead pants. They decided that they had nothing more to do so Captain Jennifer closed her little notepad and kept it beside her but Grandma Dorothy told us that there was a swimming pool in the backyard of the castle. Since we hadn't explored the castle entirely we hadn't seen the pool at all. So they had an eighth task to clean the pool and refill it. After the eight tasks they were reminded that they had to get the dirty windows cleaned. They finally made the to-do list after adding many things into it. They all realised that it was almost evening and there was no way they could go at this time so they decided to drop any plans for the day and stayed at home watching movies. They were about to have the best pad thai that Grandma was making for dinner. They all waited patiently for her to finish cooking and sat in the living room browsing for a movie to watch. Finally they decided to watch 'The Minions'. All of them had a good laugh as they enjoyed their dinner. It was so good that Alex begged Grandma Dorothy to make it everyday. They all found it funny. After dinner they played a fun game of 'Simon says' They played and played. Finally they got tired and wanted to go to sleep but they didn't know where Grandma could sleep. So Alex gave his bed to Grandma Dorothy and slept on the couch.

EIGHT

The next day they had omelettes and milk for breakfast. After breakfast and bath they were off to Hamstone City to buy cleaning agents and detergents. After buying the things they dropped it all off at the castle and went back to get gardening tools. Soon they started off with the cleaning of the castle. They grabbed their broomsticks, mops and cleaning cloth and started cleaning from the basement. After that basement they cleaned the kitchen, ball and the grand staircase. The entire day they spent cleaning the castle and by four in the evening the castle was cleaner than ever. They went home and just plopped themselves on their beds. They just ordered pizza for dinner since they were in no mood to make it. After eating their dinner they straight up refreshed and went to sleep. That night the weather turned a little cold and the next morning they just wanted to stay tucked in and they did. They stayed in bed until afternoon. They had brunch at Grandma's restaurant in Hamstone City. They had cinnamon rolls, french toast and banana pancakes. After their brunch they picked up some vegetable plant seeds to plant in the garden and also fertilisers. They went back to the castle and unloaded the things they had got. Soon they were back to work clearing out the dried, dark and dusty vegetation that had grown over the years. They were exhausted working in the sun and wanted to dive into the pool but obviously it was dirty. Nobody had touched the pool for years so they decided to add the pool cleaning water since it was probably going to take days to clear out. So they mixed the chlorine with a little bit of water and put it into the pool and left it that way. Grandma Dorothy had got a few bottles of lemonade while coming from Hamstone City, she handed them to the kids and they drank it up. They felt very refreshed and went back to work immediately. Once the place was clean they wetted the soil and dug it up a bit to mix in the pesticide and fertiliser. They planted seeds of different vegetables and made a deal that all of them will get to water the garden everyday. They rested for a while after the gardening work was done. It was almost evening and the sun was going down. The beautiful scene of the sea and sun setting was seen from the backyard. They sat in the backyard watching the sunset and after it had set completely they decided to go back home. They got into the jeep and drove off to their cottage. After refreshing they had some amazing grilled hamburgers for dinner.

NINE

They played a lot of games and watched an entire TV show that night. After their fun night they went to sleep. The dogs were already asleep in the living room's couches .The next morning they had cereal for breakfast and went to the castle. They gathered all the curtains, bedsheets and cushions and loaded them onto the jeep and gave them to the dry cleaners in Hamstone City. They hired an electrician and carpenter to fix things in the castle. They went back to the castle to find the pool in a better condition. The moss and algae had loosened up so they could just scoop it out using a net. Alex got one of those long nets and the others helped him scoop it out of the water. By the time they finished, the carpenter had come to fix things. Alex and Harry helped him with the tool box while the others just enjoyed the view from the backyard. The waves crashing onto the shore, the tiny little birds chirping, some cool breeze and the bright sun was all they needed for a perfect vacation. A while later even the electrician came so Scarlet and Jade helped him. By the end of the evening they had finished everything so they decided to take a walk by the beach. The smell of waves was just different from the heavy and smokey city air. It felt fresh and cool. A few from the group even went into the water. Just dipping their feet in. The younger ones like Katie and Caroline walked on the shore collecting seashells. Mr.Chocos tagged along behind them to make sure they didn't wander far away. The full moon was seen and it was just so peaceful that they all wished the moment never ended but unfortunately time waits for no man and they had to go back to the cottage to make dinner. They made tasty soups and salads for dinner, something light and healthy. After dinner they sat together in the living room and Alex took out a few books from his bag. He had picked up some good titles from the castle's library, one of them being the fat book fairy tales. Katie grabbed the book from Alex's hand and gave it to Grandma. She asked her to read the stories that she herself had written. They enjoyed the story and the stories made the dogs fall asleep too. Since the dogs were asleep they decided to sit in the front and stargaze. They took out a few mats and laid them on the slightly wet grass. The cool breeze was hitting their cheeks and their cheeks and nose had turned pink. They discussed that all the tasks were almost done so they just needed to get the windows cleaned. Captain Jennifer immediately called the window and glass cleaner and asked him to come the next day. After that they went in and hit the sack.

TEN

The next day they were back at the castle Scarlett and Jade were pouring water into buckets and handing them over to the window cleaners. Since they had nothing else to do they cleaned the pool entirely and had a pool party. Captain Jennifer was away at Hamstone City buying groceries to restock the castle's fridge since it had just been fixed. She came back by eleven and the kids helped her restock the fridge while some just snacked on what she got. Harry was helping Katie water the garden. Small little plant saplings were already growing and in no time they were going to have their own fresh and organic vegetable garden. They even cleaned the garage and stables so that the horses could stay with them. Everything was perfect, they couldn't have wished for a better summer vacation. Tasty food, some adventure and mystery, bright blue skies and ocean , golden sand and sun green forest and fields were just some of the things they had enjoyed that summer vacation. Before lunch they gave a nice bath to the dogs along with the horses. They really didn't even need to dive into the pool, they got wet when the horses and dogs shook themselves. After having a fun time giving a bath to the dogs and horses they wanted to have some lunch. Alex knew just what they should make for lunch. Some miso soup, sushi and ramen was ideal. So today's chef was Alex! Grandma helped him cut up seaweed, garlic and spring onions. It took some time for Alex to cook everything so Captain Jnenifer came in to help him. The lunch was ready and the kids gathered around the kitchen table and looked at the food drooling. They dug in as soon as the food was served. After dinner they rode their horses to the beach and played volleyball and made sandcastles. As they enjoyed playing, the skies suddenly became dark and it started drizzling. All of them hurried and got onto the horses and jeep and rode off to the castle. The dried themselves and lit the fireplace to warm up the place. The weather changed pretty fast but they all looked on the good side of it and decided to watch a movie. They watched 'Charlie and the Chocolate Factory' and in no less than a few minutes into the movie they all started craving chocolate. So each one of them got up and made themselves some hot chocolate and came back and continued watching the movie. After a while they ordered in some McDonalds'. After they finished dinner and the movie they had to go back to the cottage since they couldn't sleep at the castle because the sheets were at the drycleaners. They realised that the rain had stopped so they immediately rode back to the cottage before it started pouring again. As soon as they reached the cottage they hit the sack. The kids were especially tired because of all that fun they had.

ELEVEN

The next day Captain Jennifer dropped the kids off at their houses in Hamstone City so that they could spend time with their parents and she made all the improvements to the castle and it was ready for a move in. A week later the kids were back at the castle and they were going to be living there for the rest of the summer. Overjoyed, they put on some music and started dancing. Captain Jennifer and Grandma Dorothy were enjoying the show the kids had put on for them unknowingly. After having a good laugh they decide to enjoy the precious time they had left before school started again. There were only two weeks left until school so they totally got into the mood to enjoy everything they did on the vacation. They even invited their parents to come and enjoy the beautiful sea. After two weeks of enjoyment they had to get back to school. They were packing up their belongings when Ashley noticed Alex writing something in a diary. She asked him what he was doing and he answered "I'm writing a diary entry. I have been writing diary entries every night to keep a record of everything we have done. We can read it in school whenever we miss our vacation." Ashley appreciated Alex on this and felt it was a smart thing to do. Once they were all packed up they got into their respective cars and drove off with their parents and dogs to their houses. Grandma Dorothy, Captain Jennifer, Sasha and Harry waved goodbye to all of them and got into their jeep with Mr.WigglyButt and followed the others to Hamstone City. That evening everyone was telling their parents about what all they had done on their vacation. The parents were all happy that the kids had got their very much-needed break. Now they could go back to school and enjoy telling their friends about it. They all went to sleep early since there was school tomorrow and the last thought in their head before going to sleep was that they had a lot of fun and they would like to do it again.

TWELVE

The next day was the big day! They were going to meet their friends in school and not on an island. They started jumping when they saw each other during lunch. They went and hugged each other and even sat together and discussed the vacation. Even the teachers knew. It was amazing, the other kids asked a lot of questions and soon they were so popular that Alex wanted to write a novel instead of explaining so many people and so he did. At school a few weeks later there was a new girl who had transferred to their school. Alex bumped into the new girl during lunch and they instantly became friends. Her name was Amber, she was a sassy and athletic girl. Over the school year they became very good friends and during the next summer vacation Alex invited her over to the castle. Since they all travelled around on horses on the island Amber too needed one so Captain Jennifer gave hers to Amber since she always brings the dogs in her jeep and so they all enjoyed riding their horses along the seashore. Amber had taken some time to blend in with the group but she still stood out at the same time. They all loved their new friend and helped her in getting to know their horses better and even gave her a major tour of the castle and island. Alex and Amber loved cycling so while they were cycling in Hamstone City they found a little puppy that was extremely sick. They got it to the vet and the vet told them that she had been starving for a long time and it was best if they took her home and first gave her something to eat. Alex took her to his house with Amber and fed her well before taking her to the castle. He asked his mother to drop him off at the castle with Amber. During the ride, the little pup had fallen asleep and both the kids were deciding a nickname for her. They decided to name her Lian which means 'delicate' in Mandarin since they found her in a very fragile and feeble condition. When they got to the castle they gave her a nice bath and put her to sleep. The other dogs were very curious to meet her but she needed to take rest so that she could recover and meet the others! Alex and Paris decided to keep Lian as their own dog. When Alex finished writing his book, Grandma Dorothy helped him publish it since she had a lot of contacts. Once the book was published everyone in the school had read it and the book's name just happened to be 'Kibble Krew and the Castle on North Hill'.

THIRTEEN

Once his book got published, everybody read it and loved the story. With the success of Alex's book and the castle being found they decided to have a party by the beach!How fun is that? They decorated the place by putting fairy lights and balloons. They even assembled their tents. They had music, drinks, food,games, the waves of the sea and of course the beautiful sunset. It was perfect Alex was the DJ along with Amber and he had chosen amazing songs that gave summer vibes. All the girls wore flowy white frocks and the boys stuck on with their tank tops and swimming trunks. Before the sun went down they all took a dip in the ocean. They enjoyed it until Grandma Dorothy arrived at the party. She had been in Hamstone City and so Captain Jennifer decided to invite her. The kids ran to hug Grandma! They played beach volleyball for a while and then all of them gathered around the grill where Captain Jennifer was grilling some veggie patties for their burgers. As the patties cooked one by one, they started their party. The music was on, the drinks were poured and they were dancing. Paris was amazing at dancing and ever since they started planning the party she even taught Alex many dances and surprisingly Alex was pretty good at dancing. But he got tired of dancing and took over the DJ with Amber. It was Amber's turn to dance so she went and started dancing hilariously. After their dances they sat together around the bonfire and made their burgers. Everything was fresh from their vegetable garden in the castle. The dogs also were enjoying themselves chasing the waves for a while and resting and doing the same again. Mr.WigglyButt even stole a carrot from the vegetable garden and he had got it to the beach to play with. After dinner they played a game of ball to entertain the dogs. Tired from playing and enjoying themselves so much they sat down and Captain Jennifer handed each of them a skewer and took out yet another bag of marshmallows. They put the marshmallows on the skewers and started roasting them over the fire and it all felt like the first time before they found the castle except that now they were living in the castle with a new friend. The dogs had been playing their own little game of hide and seek by digging up the sand and hiding the toys they had got. It was late night and the moon and stars were shining brightly. They started stargazing and the dogs also got tired and fell asleep. At last they fell asleep on the beach itself.

FOURTEEN

The following morning they woke up to the bright sun and went to Hamstone City to grab the craziest breakfast. Twelve large cups of ice cream! Actually sixteen large cups of ice cream. The dogs enjoyed their crazy breakfast too! On the way back they grabbed cold drinks and snacks. To the beach they drove and they planned on enjoying the sea waters for the entire day. They had their floater and as soon as they reached the sand they jumped right into the water. It was warm but enjoyable. After playing for a while in the water they came out and played 'Tag'. Captain Jennifer and Grandma Dorothy were relaxing and talking to each other. The dog were still having fun in the water and Mr.Chocos even caught a poor fish but let it go. They started getting a bit bored so they decided to ride their horses. It was so fun that they rode their horses around with the dogs running behind them until afternoon. Grandma surprised the kids with their favourite pesto pasta that they cooked together last time. Alex was very pleased that Grandma kept her promise. Just when they finished their lunch Ashley grabbed Alex's bag and took out his diary that he had written when they found the castle. They decided to read together. Everyone was surprised at how detailed everything was. All of them appreciated Alex and went to make sand castles. They all made the biggest sandcastle ever. Lian, who was new to all of this, decided to destroy the sandcastle by running right into it. The castle collapsed right on top of her. Worried Amber rushed to see if Lian was fun but Lian looked pretty satisfied with what she had done. Alex started laughing at Amber but he appreciated her caring nature towards the things she loves. It was almost evening and it started getting really boring so they had the best idea ever! They decided to call everyone's parents!!! The more people, the more fun. They all got their phones and sent messages to each of their parents and invited them to their little beach party. In no time the parents started arriving one by one with some ingredients for yet another grill party.

FIFTEEN

Once all the parents arrived they lit the bonfire again and made dinner. The women matched their dresses with the kids and the men again stuck on with their trunks and tank tops. The men grilled some amazing steak and brought it to the long table they had assembled. They sat together and joked until their dinner was over. After dinner they played hide and seek. It was fun since the dogs also took part. After the game the adults sat down for drinks while the kids played with the dogs. Caroline and Katie were busy trying to find shells but they accidentally found a bunch of crabs and came screaming to their parents. They found the crabs and drove them away but Alex and Amber who were now known as the 'daredevils' proceeded to pick up crabs like they were stones and they even petted them. The parents started laughing at this. After tossing the crabs back into the sea, they found some jellyfish. Alex plopped the jellyfish back in and walked back to their party spot. Amber ran behind the disco and played the music. Everyone gathered and danced the night away.

Vibha Chethan is a curious teen and a pet ethusiast. She loves animals. Spending time and playing with animals is something she enjoys greatly. Writing a book was something Vibha hadn't even thought of until the pandemic started. As she started writing the story her artistic mind and creative instincts were exposed. Taking inspiration from little things and adding them into her creative scenarios was something she enjoyed while writing this story. From naming the characters to coming up with concepts, she always made sure to ask her friend Captain Jennifer for inputs.Her friends were a great source of inspiration but as a teen watching movies and TV shows also helped spark her artistic mind. Lastly, she knew just how to use the pandemic to her advantage.

www.ingramcontent.com/pod-product-compliance
Lightning Source LLC
Chambersburg PA
CBHW031721180726
47993CB00022B/1591